See me run.
I run and run.

See them come.
They come and come.

Will they get me?
No, no, no!
We go and go.

Now I stop.
What is this?

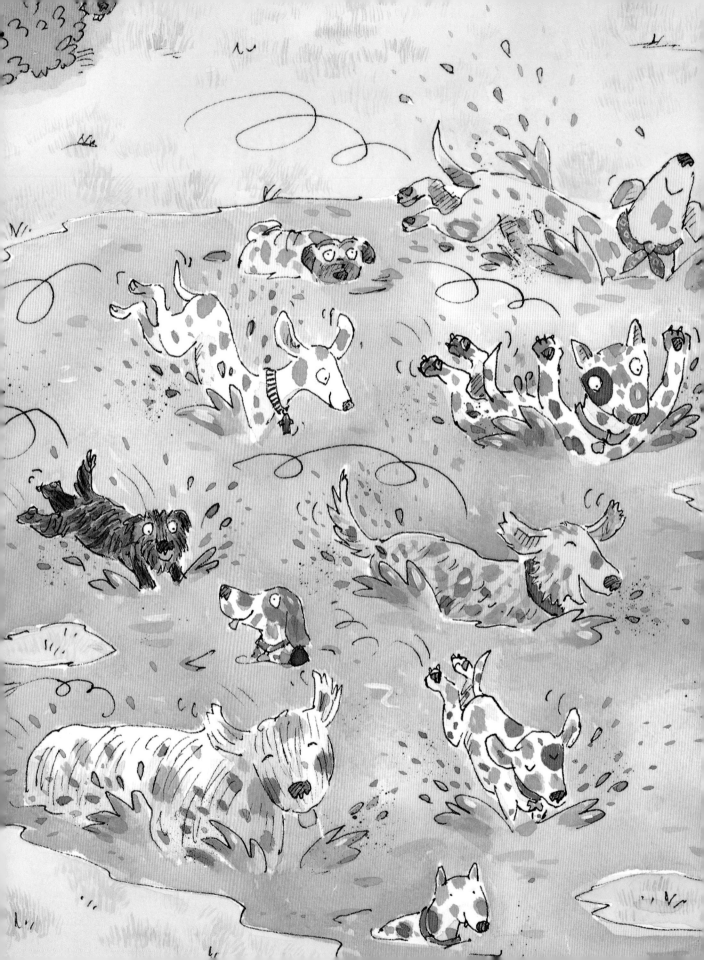

It is mud.
Splat-splat.
Mud is fun.

We need a bath.
Splash-splash.
A bath is fun.

See me dig.

We all dig.

We dig and dig and dig and dig.

What is this?

It is big.

It is mad.

And now we run again!